W9-BQI-373

OHIO
DOMINICAN
UNIVERSITY™

SINCE 1911

IN MEMORY OF

Theresa King

The Collector of Moments

Buchholz
chholz, Quint.
e collector of moments

QUINT BUCHHOLZ

The Collector of Moments

Translated from the German by Peter F. Neumeyer

FARRAR, STRAUS AND GIROUX ◆ NEW YORK

Text and pictures copyright © 1997 by Carl Hanser Verlag
Translation copyright © 1999 by Farrar, Straus and Giroux
All rights reserved
Distributed in Canada by Douglas & McIntyre Ltd.
First published in Germany by Carl Hanser Verlag, 1997
Printed in Germany
First American edition, 1999

Library of Congress Cataloging-in-Publication Data
Buchholz, Quint.
    [Sammler der Augenblicke.   English.]
    The collector of moments / Quint Buchholz ; translated from
the German by Peter F. Neumeyer. — 1st American ed.
       p.   cm.
    Summary: When Max, an artist, departs for a long journey,
the boy who is his friend and neighbor visits his apartment and
discovers an exhibition of pictures created just for him.
    ISBN 0-374-31520-5
    [1. Artists—Fiction.]   I. Neumeyer, Peter F., 1929– .
II. Title
PZ7.B87732Co   1999
[Fic]—dc21   99-10202

To my mother

At dusk, when he couldn't draw anymore, Max used to sing.

In a rumpled black linen jacket, he would stand by the window of the studio and sing.

You could see the ocean between the houses on the other side of the street. Far out, beyond the harbor wall, the lighthouse beacon would begin to blink. You could see the ferry as it made the day's last crossing from the mainland. It drew a thin banner of smoke across the skies, and a flight of seagulls followed behind.

Max sang with a clear, almost childlike voice. His songs were wordless.

I'd snuggle into the cozy red easy chair and listen.

One day Max heard me play the violin.

From that time on, every evening he'd ask me to play while he sang.

Or sometimes he'd merely listen to my playing.

"You do make beautiful music, Professor," he'd say when we were through. He always called me that.

In school, I was often teased for my old-fashioned wire-rimmed glasses, and because I was a bit heavy. But when Max called me "Professor," he sounded friendly and appreciative.

I'd pack up my violin and run down the two flights to my parents', for dinner.

We lived in an apartment on Harbor Street, a wide street which coursed through the city and down to the ferry landing in the harbor.

Downstairs, my father had his store. On the sign above the entrance, scrolled, dark blue letters spelled out *Ironworks*, and below that, in smaller writing, PROPRIETOR, E. BUCHHOLZ.

The people of the island bought hardware from him—hinges, joints, door locks, screws and nails of all sizes and shapes.

Our apartment was directly above the store. I shared a room with my older brother.

One warm March day, Max moved in above us, on the fourth floor.

The first herring gulls had returned from the south, and they filled the air with their screams. The wind scudded small white clouds across the sky and wafted the scent of saltwater up from the sea.

A yellow furniture van stood in the sun, in front of our house. Men in blue overalls carried moving cartons upstairs—tables, chairs, bookshelves, flower pots, an old globe, an easel, and a dark red velvet easy chair.

Max hurried back and forth among the men, giving directions and running a hand through his blond hair.

He stayed through the summer, through the winter, and through the next summer. Then, with the approach of autumn, he went away.

A small stairway with worn and creaking steps and a wrought-iron railing led to the fourth floor. Almost every day, I would stand in the gray-painted entrance and carefully try the door.

If the place was not locked up, I was allowed to visit.

❖   ❖   ❖

Often I would spend whole afternoons in his study as Max worked on his pictures. Lying on my stomach on the dark plank floor, I would do my homework. Or, on large sheets of Max's sketching paper, I'd draw sailboats in a storm, brave Indian chiefs, knights fighting, and fire-spewing dragons. Or I'd construct cardboard and tinfoil rockets powered by match heads. I would capture flies to be the travelers aboard my manned space flight, which was to take off from the city park. I would read *Robinson Crusoe*, *Treasure Island*, or *Big Tiger and Christian*, books that I found on Max's crowded shelves. Heavy picture books were piled up all over the floor. I disappeared into bygone worlds of kings and queens, followed the tracks of explorers and the migrations of wild animals, visited distant cities and countries, and saw the works of famous builders and distinguished painters.

Knowing that I would always win, I played chess against myself.

Occasionally, I would travel the world on the old globe which stood on a stool next to the oil stove, and my index finger would leave the tracks of my journeys in the dust that covered the Northern Hemisphere.

The muffled sounds of the street would drift up. Sometimes you would hear the whistle of the ferry from the harbor. On hot summer days, the fan on the ceiling would hum. The clock on the wall ticked away, and I would hear the regular, gentle scratching of Max's drawing pen on the paper.

For hours he would sit almost immobile at the large table, surrounded by pages of sketches, books, pencils, and countless jars of colored inks. His upper body was bent over his picture, and the hand with the pen moved slowly and repeatedly across the paper in small, calm movements.

Occasionally he'd wipe the pen with an old spotted rag, place the picture on its easel next to the table, and consider it for a long time. He'd brush a hand through his hair. And sometimes a smile would flicker across his face. Usually, though, his brow would be deeply furrowed.

Sometimes, too, he'd stand up, pace restlessly back and forth in the studio, look out the window, or disappear for a time into the kitchen.

Then he'd sit down at the table again, take his picture from the easel, and continue to work.

I used to love to watch Max from my red easy chair, even though I could not see what it was he was drawing. He was secretive about his pictures. While he was working, I was never permitted to look.

And weeks later, when a picture was finished, it would be placed in a white frame and set against the wall, next to other pictures, back side facing out.

"One invisible and unique path leads into every picture," Max said once, "and the artist has to find just that one path. He can't show the picture too soon, or he might lose that path forever."

✦   ✦   ✦

Often, Max would journey outdoors. He would crisscross the city streets like an explorer, run along the broad beach or over the dunes, hair streaming, jacket blown open by the wind.

He could sit in silence for many hours on the harbor wall, on a bench in the park, or at a café on the promenade. His gaze was fixed on the distance, as though he was searching for something there.

Sometimes I'd see him take notes or make quick sketches in a little book he always carried with him.

At other times, he'd go on longer voyages. I'd accompany him down to the dock and then would run out on the breakwater, to the lighthouse. When the ferry passed, Max would be standing by the railing at the stern, with his brown suitcase, waving. I, too, waved, and followed him with my eyes until the ferry was only a tiny dot on the horizon.

✦ ✦ ✦

He never told me when he would return. Perhaps, at the time of his departure, he didn't even know.

But there would come a time when the door to his lodgings was not locked anymore. I could enter just as before. Max would look up from the table and wink at me, and then withdraw into a new picture.

And again the wonderful peace of the room would envelop me, and I would settle into the red chair.

At dusk, as always, I'd play my violin. Max would sing along. Or he would be silent.

Seldom would Max talk about his travels.

However, when he did talk about them, he would relate curious tales, things and events which I'd never heard of before.

One winter day, Max stopped drawing earlier than usual. We sat together at the window in the studio and drank tea out of dark blue cups. Outside, it was snowing heavily, and everything seemed even quieter than usual.

"Did you know that in Canada there are snow elephants?" Max asked, both our glances following the falling snowflakes. "They're even bigger than African elephants, and they have thick white fur—sort of like polar bears. They're very shy and they come out of the woods only in fierce blizzards. Even though they are so large, they move quietly and gracefully. Only very rarely can you see them pass by. And usually, before you've had a chance to look closely, they've already disappeared into the blowing snow."

For a while, we looked out the window in silence. Then Max told about a flying circus wagon which he'd seen once, late in the evening, when he had gone for a stroll in a small French town. With lit-up windows, the circus wagon hovered silently in the sky, then floated across a bridge and slowly disappeared into the dark of night.

I liked these stories. They sounded so implausible, and yet Max recounted them as though he really had seen all these things. Of course I wanted him to tell me the truth.

"Come on, let's make music, Professor," he said with a smile, and carried the teacups into the kitchen. There were times when he just did not want to explain what was most important.

Max had now lived in our house for more than a year.

And in that time he had leaned a long row of pictures, back side facing out, against the walls of the studio.

One evening, when once again in the dusk we had made our music, Max said he must go away for a longer time. He handed me a bunch of keys and asked me to look after his home while he was away, to water the flowers and take in the mail.

The best part, though, was that he allowed me to be in the studio any time I wanted.

Max left on a cool morning at the beginning of summer vacation, and I accompanied him down to the dock.

Patches of soft mist hung over the water, and the early-morning sunlight glittered on the curling waves. As usual, I was standing by the lighthouse and waved to Max as the ferry went by. A gull flew low over my head, screeching. Way out to sea, two sailboats crossed on the silvery water.

I ran back along the harbor wall and past the beach hotels and street cafés, where waiters were straightening chairs and wiping tables. Colored umbrellas were fluttering in the wind. At the corner of the harbor street, a hurdy-gurdy man was grinding out a song.

There were letters in Max's mailbox. I took them out and ran upstairs.

My heart was beating as I opened his front door.

The hallway was in gloom. Max had set the flower pots all together on the kitchen table. I put the letters next to them.

The door to the studio was open. The clock on the wall was ticking.

Hesitantly, I entered. Behind the lowered shades, the sunlight fell on the floor in thin stripes.

Something had changed. The pictures were still standing against the wall in a long row. But now they were looking at me.

Now I was intended to see them. Now I was permitted.

In front of each picture was a piece of sketching paper on which Max had written a message.

I stood in the middle of an exhibition which he had assembled just for me.

More in the foreground, in the shade of a chestnut tree, an old lady pointed the way for visitors.

Snow elephants in Canada.
It lasts just for the blink of an eye.

One January 1.
It had been snowing all night.

The evening before, the circus had given its farewell performance.

Once again, the street was empty
and deserted. A moment later,
a taxi came around the corner.

In the morning, at half past six.
A dog barked in the house, and
someone turned on the light.

The narrow stripes of sunlight passed slowly over the floorboards. Time, in Max's pictures, seemed to stretch out into infinity.

In the silence of the studio, I squatted on the floor, letting my eyes glide endlessly over all these curious things that Max had created.

I wanted to ask him so many things. Perhaps these pictures were memories of things he had seen on his travels. Now, as they passed by, I saw the snow elephants he had told me about. I recognized the hovering circus wagon as well.

Everything had been drawn in great detail and seemed familiar to me—even the colors: the cool blue of the snow, the shimmering green of the meadows in the morning sun, the glowing yellow of lights in the night. And still, in every picture, something unusual was taking place. Happenings that confused me and mesmerized me and almost pulled me into the picture.

Max always captured a precise moment. But I understood that there was always a story attached to this moment which had begun long before and would continue long afterward.

In one picture I saw a giant package standing next to a house. But I could not tell how it got there, what was packed inside, or whom the cows were looking at. Max had not captured those things.

Once, he said something which, at the time, I had not understood: "Every picture has a secret to keep. Even from me. Others might actually discover much more in my pictures than I do." And then he added, "I'm merely the collector. I collect moments."

Now I began to see what he had meant by that.

In a mirror next to a doorway that led to the beach, Max had depicted himself. His brown suitcase with the brass clasps sat by the door. Next to it lay his sketchbook. On the scrap of paper in front of the picture I read: "The Collector of Moments."

Sometimes children would pass,
discuss something with the man,
and then disappear behind
one of the doors.

They flew in the direction of the coast. A deep, breathy tone sounded into the night.

During the day, the man worked in the office of a railroad company.

On the nearby hill, there was a castle with white windows.

They stood there for a long time,
talking together, before they went on.

In the following weeks, whenever I'd visit the studio, I would set up a different picture for myself on the easel, which I had carried over to my red chair by the window.

Then I'd undertake ever new travels to all those places which Max had created for me. I would go through mysterious doors and would wander through nighttime streets. Alongside the chickens, I'd stomp through snowy landscapes and listen to the big fellow and the little one there by the ocean. With the clown and the goose I'd run across meadows, and with the penguins I'd run through the city. Sometimes I'd be the king, at other times I'd be the little girl, as I navigated across the waters with the lion.

On every one of these trips, I'd have different experiences, and setting forth from any one of the pictures, I could go to different places. And when I had come back from the pictures, there would be the soft pillow of the chair, the soothing ticks of the clock on the wall, and the security of the room itself.

Slowly it began to dawn on me why I was to look at the pictures while Max was away. He had not wanted to be present to have to give me explanations. The answers to all my questions were revealed in the long spells which I spent in front of the pictures.

Summer vacation was over.

Finally, the picture with the lighthouse was on the easel. Even though I saw the lighthouse of our island almost every day, never ever had I seen it as Max had drawn it in the mist.

I fetched my violin and tried to play the music I heard coming out of the picture. It became a soft, cheerful melody.

And on this evening, outside too, in front of the window, the city almost disappeared in the dense fog, and the ocean was not to be seen.

Max's scrap of paper said only: "Lighthouse on an island." I turned it over and wrote on the back: "The horse is hard of hearing, Max, but I hear the music clearly."

Next morning, Max returned on the first ferry, and everything changed.

On his trip, he had found a house in the south, far from our island.

How was I to comprehend that he wanted to move away? He had come here to live with us, looking for a place where he could peacefully create all those pictures which had now been entrusted to me.

But he told me that he was never able to remain in the same place for long. He said that now, since there were no more pictures to do here, his time on the island was over. He said he had to go somewhere else and there he would make new, perhaps entirely different kinds of pictures.

And then he added that the time spent with me had been very good, that I was a very special person and, by all means, I should continue to make music.

Never before had Max talked to me that way.

I listened. But I did not understand.

Summer had passed.

Gray mountains of clouds towered in the heavens and the churned-up waters were dark brown.

We were standing at the pier. My parents and my brother had come along to the harbor with us.

Max set down his brown suitcase and ran a hand through his hair. His black jacket fluttered in the wind which was lashing up from the ocean, across the island, driving leaves and twigs along the pavement.

In the row of cars which were waiting for the ferry, there was a yellow furniture van.

For the last time, I heard Max's warm voice. "I'll miss you, Professor," he said softly, and I looked down at my shoes.

Then he crossed the rusty ramp to the ferry.

On this day, I did not run down to the lighthouse.

For a long time, we waved at the departing Max.

The wind blew sea froth across the harbor wall and sprayed us. I was no longer able to see through the lenses of my glasses. I simply stood there in my wet blue anorak. The seawater tasted salty, like tears, and I felt my mother's hand on my shoulder.

A fat couple with a young boy and a tiny dog who barked all day moved into Max's place.

In exchange for a string of licorice, the boy would occasionally let me pedal his new bicycle with its shiny chrome. He would show me his toy car track and his large collection of plastic rocket ships. I did not tell him about the plans for my rockets.

We played football in the park, and we'd let our kites fly on the beach, in the cold wind. For a long time, I did not touch my violin. When I unpacked it for the first time, my brother gave a sigh of concern.

Occasionally, when the ferry came from the mainland, I would run out to the lighthouse, and looking into the bright light, I would try to discern the faces of the travelers leaning against the front railing.

Winter passed. And then, on a warm March day, a package arrived from Max. Brightly colored foreign stamps were pasted on the wrapping paper.

Inside the package there was a picture: On a harbor wall, surrounded by pictures, there stands a red easy chair. Gulls glide over the glittering water. Sailboats pass in the distance. A boy in a blue anorak is standing on the chair, playing the violin. He is wearing old-fashioned wire-rimmed glasses, and he's a little heavy.

On the back of the picture is pasted a torn-out piece of

sketching paper. And there, in Max's large, familiar pencil writing, are the words: "You know something, Professor—your music is always there in my pictures."

Max's picture now hangs in the hallway of our house, right by the door to my little daughter's room. I look at it every morning as I take my coat off the hook. Then I take the streetcar to the School of Music, where I teach my violin students.

◆　　◆　　◆

QUINT BUCHHOLZ was born in Stolberg, Germany, in 1957, and grew up in Stuttgart. He turned to illustrating at the age of sixteen, "because in pictures I could express things I couldn't talk about—that was the reason I started." He studied art history, painting, and graphics at the Munich Academy of Art and began illustrating professionally in 1980. Mr. Buchholz lives with his wife and three children in Ottobrunn, near Munich.

PETER F. NEUMEYER is the author of a half-dozen books for children, a volume of poetry, *The Annotated "Charlotte's Web"*, and scholarly studies ranging from Shakespeare to Kafka. Currently, he is monthly children's book reviewer for *The Boston Globe*. He lives with his wife in Kensington, California.

DATE DUE